FIVE LADIES IN SEARCH OF HAPPINESS

RIDDHIMA

To every woman who has ever paused her dreams, whispered her truth in silence, or carried the weight of others with grace. This is for you. May you find your happiness, unapologetically.

Contents

In a world constantly asking women to choose between their ambition and affection, independence and duty, identity and expectation, ***Five Ladies In Search of Happiness*** is a fictional yet deeply resonant journey of reconnection. These pages offer not just stories but mirrors—reflecting the ache, the resilience, and the rediscovery of self. This book is an invitation to listen to the parts of you that have been waiting to speak.

Preface

This story was born from a question I found myself asking repeatedly: what does happiness really mean for women who have given so much of themselves to others? These five characters—Serenya, Liora, Nyra, Virelle, and Caela—emerged as a response. They are entirely fictional, but their desires, fears, and courage are drawn from the unspoken stories I've encountered in conversations, silence, and introspection. Through these intertwined narratives, I hope readers see not just the women on these pages, but also themselves.

Acknowledgements

To the storytellers, quiet warriors, and soul-searchers who inspired the voices in this book—thank you. To my early readers and confidants who encouraged this idea when it was nothing more than a scribble—your faith carried me through. And to every woman who ever dared to choose herself—you are the reason this story exists.

Prologue

Happiness is a word whispered in dreams, scribbled in journals, chased down winding roads, and sometimes—found in the unlikeliest of places. This is the story of five women, strangers to each other at first, who cross paths by fate and choose to walk together toward something they all yearn for: happiness.

1

Serenya – The Silent Song

Serenya Vale had once been a rising star in the world of classical music. Her haunting voice could silence the noisiest halls, her compositions praised by maestros. But now, in the city of Amarinth, she lived in the shadow of her former self.

Every morning, she prepared herbal tea for her ailing mother, Ilena, who was bedridden and sharp-tongued.

"You should've been married by now," Ilena grumbled from the daybed. "All that singing, what did it get you?"

Serenya stirred the tea in silence. "Peace, Ma. It gave me peace."

The apartment was dim, filled with dust-coated trophies and faded newspaper clippings. Serenya rarely sang now. The music room had become storage, her tanpura left untouched, covered in a muslin cloth.

One afternoon, she opened her inbox and saw the message:

Invitation: Celestine Music Festival, Prague
We would be honored to feature Serenya Vale as a soloist...

Her breath caught. Her hands trembled. Prague. The dream she'd buried.

"Ma," she whispered later that evening, "What if I traveled? Just for a short while."

Ilena's eyes narrowed. "Leave me here to rot? Is that what you want?"

Serenya turned to the window. Outside, the rain played a rhythm only she could hear. "I want to remember who I was. Before the silence."

Ilena said nothing.

That night, Serenya opened her music notebook. Her fingers, uncertain at first, began tracing notes on the page. A melody formed. A new song, born from years of quiet yearning.

And in that moment, she decided. She would go.

2

Liora – The Mirror's Lie

❦

Liora Kade was the face of Aurum, the most iconic fashion magazine in Aerinth City. Every glossy cover, every daring editorial, carried her signature style—elegant, fierce, unapologetic. People saw her as a woman who had it all.

But behind her mirrored office walls, the truth was far from perfect.

"I'm sorry, Liora, but this look—it's too safe. We're losing edge," barked a young assistant during the weekly design review.

Liora raised a sharp brow. "Then push it. But don't confuse edge with chaos."

Her tone was ice, but inside, she was unraveling. The pressure, the pace, the constant scrutiny—it had chipped away at her for years. At night, she'd sit in her penthouse, remove her makeup, and stare into the mirror.

"Who even are you without all this?" she whispered to her reflection.

The answer never came.

Then came the breaking point.

During Aerinth Fashion Week, as flashbulbs flared and models paraded in gold-threaded gowns, Liora froze backstage. Her breath vanished. Her vision blurred.

She collapsed.

Diagnosed with burnout and anxiety, she was forced to take medical leave.

"Get away," her therapist said. "Not to a spa. Not to another fashion capital. Somewhere quiet. Somewhere unknown."

Liora booked a one-way ticket to the Snowspire Mountains. She found a small lodge in the village of Velwyth, surrounded by frost-tipped pines and silence thick enough to choke thoughts.

The first few days were torment. No phone. No laptop. Just journals, cold air, and the ache of withdrawal—from the spotlight, from validation.

One night, while walking a trail lined with fireflies, she met a woman named Anwyn, an herbalist who lived nearby.

"You look like someone who's forgotten how to breathe," Anwyn said.

"I used to run a world. Now I can't run from my own head," Liora confessed.

Anwyn smiled gently. "Then stop running. Be still. Let yourself fall apart. That's when the truth slips in."

That night, Liora wrote for hours. Not press releases or interviews. Just... truths. Ugly, raw, and necessary.

She wasn't healed. But for the first time, she felt human.

3

Nyra - The Unseen Revolution

Nyra Solis lived in the modest village of Dalkhera, tucked deep in the cliffs of southern Valmira. Her life as a schoolteacher was steady—morning lessons, evening chai, the occasional visit to her brother's farm. But there was more to Nyra than dusty chalkboards and children's rhymes.

By night, under the guise of anonymity, she penned fiercely honest columns about gender, caste, and inequality. Her words, signed under the pseudonym "Vermilion Fire," stirred conversations across the nation. Yet no one in Dalkhera suspected that the quiet woman in simple saris was the voice rattling elite columns and parliamentary debate.

Her only confidant was her elderly neighbor, Master Rilu.

"You still hiding from your own fire, girl?" he asked one evening, watching her burn a draft.

"I can't risk them finding out," she said. "If they know, I lose my job. Maybe more."

Rilu handed her a letter, eyes twinkling. "Someone sent this to my address, asking for you. Thought you might want to read it."

Nyra unfolded the parchment, heart racing.

Your writing is a spark the world needs. We are organizing a retreat for women who wish to reclaim their voice. The location is secret. You'll be safe.

Come, if you're ready to stop hiding.

She stared at the signature—no name, just a symbol. A quill aflame.

She spent the night walking the orchard behind her house, wind whispering through the banyan trees.

"Nyra," she murmured to herself, "what do you stand for if not your truth?"

In the morning, she called the school principal.

"Sir, I'd like to apply for a short sabbatical. For… health reasons."

He sighed. "Take care of yourself, Ms. Solis. You've earned it."

By the end of the week, Nyra had packed a satchel with her notebooks, shawls, and a folded scarf embroidered with the symbol of the quill aflame.

She didn't know where she was going. But she knew why.

4

Virelle – The Road Not Taken

Virelle Aster had once dreamed of cartography—of sketching the veins of mountains, tracing paths across continents. But instead, she found herself buried in spreadsheets and beige cubicles, working for a logistics firm in Greynor.

At thirty-eight, she was the dependable one. The fixer. The aunt who remembered birthdays, the sister who wired money when her brother gambled it away, the coworker who covered shifts during holidays.

She smiled a lot. But no one saw how often her hands trembled at night.

"You okay, Vee?" her manager asked one evening.

She nodded too quickly. "Just tired. Just—tired."

Her apartment was small, filled with plants and maps of places she had never visited.

One night, she received a message from an old friend, Eliran, who had once shared her love for geography.

Found something you'd love. Abandoned trail near the Marrowridge Cliffs. They say it disappears into fog and

reappears somewhere else. Wanna find it?

Something about it tugged at her. A trail that vanished. Like her.

She called her manager the next morning.

"I'm cashing in my leave. All of it."

She packed her boots, her maps, her journal, and took a train east. The Marrowridge Cliffs were shrouded in silence. The trail began as a footpath, then twisted into mist and moss. She followed it.

Along the way, she met a group of women—travelers, seekers, quiet wanderers like herself. They invited her to join their fire.

"What are you looking for?" one of them asked.

Virelle looked up at the stars. "I'm not sure. But I think it's something I lost a long time ago."

A pause. Then she added, "Maybe it's me."

She stayed with them for days, then weeks. They spoke little, but when they did, it mattered. One morning, she opened her journal and began sketching the trail—her trail.

For the first time in decades, she was mapping again.

And in every line, she began to rediscover the woman she had once set aside.

5

Caela – The Sky Within

Caela Vionn had always felt at home in the skies.

As a child in the coastal town of Liraen, she would climb onto the roof of her family's bakery and lie back for hours, watching clouds tumble past like caravans. She could name every kind of bird, trace constellations with her fingers, and dream of far-off worlds. But dreams had a way of grounding themselves in reality.

After her father died, Caela stayed behind to run the bakery with her mother. Yeast replaced textbooks. Dough replaced daydreams. She worked before dawn, kneading, shaping, baking, smiling for customers. Her mother, once vibrant, now moved like a ghost of grief.

"You're the strong one," people would say. "Liraen would fall apart without the Vionn girls."

Caela would nod. Smile. Go back to kneading.

But when the ovens cooled and silence fell, she'd retreat to the attic. There, she kept an old telescope, a faded map of the sky, and a worn journal filled with questions she had no time to ask.

One evening, a stranger walked into the bakery. Tall, with sand in her hair and a satchel slung over her shoulder.

"Starberry tart," she said, smiling. "Used to eat one every time I passed through here. Is your father around?"

Caela blinked. "No. I run it now."

The woman's eyes softened. "He once told me you had the mind of a sky-walker. Always watching the stars."

Caela gave a quiet laugh. "That girl got buried under flour years ago."

Before leaving, the woman handed her a small envelope.

"The Sky Within – A gathering of women who still remember how to wonder. You are invited."
Coordinates enclosed. No explanations. Just come.

For days, Caela stared at the envelope. She tucked it in her apron. Read it under moonlight. Ignored it. Read it again.

Finally, she sat across from her mother at the kitchen table.

"I want to go," she said softly. "Not forever. Just… enough."

Her mother didn't look up from her tea. "Your father used to say you'd fly one day."

Caela held her breath.

"Don't wait until your wings forget how."

And so, she went.

She followed the coordinates through dusty roads, across ferry lines, and into highlands where the stars felt close enough to kiss. The retreat sat atop a ridge, a circle of domed shelters and firelit paths. Women gathered here—not broken, not whole, just seeking.

There, she met others like her—Serenya, Liora, Nyra, Virelle—each carrying fragments of themselves, each drawn by something unnamed.

Under the endless sky, Caela lay back once more. For the first time in years, she didn't feel guilty for dreaming.

And she remembered: she had never stopped being a sky-walker.

Just... paused.

Caela Vireth had always lived in the clouds—literally and figuratively. As a commercial pilot for SkyArc Airlines, her life was flight schedules, navigation charts, and hotel check-ins in faraway cities. But even soaring at 30,000 feet, she could never escape the weight of her own heart.

She had loved once. Deeply. A woman named Selene who painted skies in watercolor and saw Caela as more than the uniform she wore. But Selene had moved on—married, settled, unreachable.

And Caela? She kept flying, her smile a mask, her silence a refuge.

One rainy evening, grounded in Liorra City due to a mechanical delay, Caela sat alone at an airport lounge watching a little girl press her face to the window.

"You waiting on someone?" Caela asked.

"My mama," the girl replied. "She says planes bring people home."

That night, the words stuck with Caela.

When she returned to her hotel, she opened her flight bag and removed a photo—Selene, laughing under a stormy sky, paint on her cheeks. Beneath it, a note Selene once wrote: Find your sky. The one inside you.

Caela wept. Not from regret, but release.

A week later, she requested a month's leave—something she'd never done. She flew, not to work, but to the Isle of Thireen, a quiet place they once dreamed of visiting together.

There, she didn't fly. She walked.

She met a woman named Nyra, who was reading poetry beneath a fig tree. Later that week, she crossed paths with a soft-spoken traveler named Virelle. Then came Serenya, humming as she journaled, and Liora, sketching fireflies in a notebook.

They had all come to this strange, quiet isle—drawn by some invisible tether of longing.

One night, seated around a crackling fire under a starlit sky, Caela looked around and whispered,

"Maybe... maybe happiness isn't a destination. Maybe it's who we meet on the way."

The women nodded, silent in agreement.

Each had traveled a different road, but they had arrived together.

And in the sharing of their stories, they found something they never expected—belonging.

Not the end. Just the beginning.

The retreat's final evening came with a quiet hum. Lanterns danced gently in the wind, their golden glow swaying over firelit conversations and the scent of salt carried from the cliffs beyond. Serenya, Liora, Nyra, Virelle, and Caela sat in a circle beneath a sprawling tree they had nicknamed "The Witness."

No one said much at first. Silence had become their language. Shared glances. Smiles that knew. Scars that no longer needed to be explained.

Virelle looked around. "Do you ever think we were meant to meet?"

Liora chuckled softly. "Only every day."

Nyra leaned back, arms tucked behind her head. "It's strange, isn't it? How we came here searching for something—and ended up finding each other."

Serenya, voice still as soft as morning mist, added, "And ourselves. Bit by bit."

Caela opened her notebook, the one she'd once hidden in an attic. She passed it around. Each page held a sketch, a quote, a memory—pieces of their time together.

"I think happiness," she said, "was never about one big moment. It was all of this. The little choices. The courage to leave. The trust to stay."

The wind picked up. Above them, stars blinked into view.

That night, they didn't sleep. They talked. Laughed. Cried. They wrote letters to their former selves and set them alight in a ceremonial fire, watching the flames carry old burdens skyward.

When morning broke, they walked down the path together, not as seekers, but as women who had found something—if not everything—they came for. Not an end. A beginning.

Happiness, they learned, wasn't a destination. It was a choice. A journey. A home they carried within.

And now, they were finally ready to live it.